Avoiding Confrontations By Writing Poetry

By
Victoria Hasenauer

Bloomington, IN Milton Keynes, UK

authorHOUSE™

AuthorHouse™
1663 Liberty Drive, Suite 200
Bloomington, IN 47403
www.authorhouse.com
Phone: 1-800-839-8640

AuthorHouse™ UK Ltd.
500 Avebury Boulevard
Central Milton Keynes, MK9 2BE
www.authorhouse.co.uk
Phone: 08001974150

First published by AuthorHouse 2/13/2006

ISBN: 1-4208-0866-4 (e)
ISBN: 1-4208-0865-6 (sc)

Printed in the United States of America
Bloomington, Indiana

This book is printed on acid-free paper.

For
my family and best friends
To
my children;
may God's plan convey illumination

Table of Contents

I. Nature

Black Secret.. 2

The Internal Bang of Spring.. 3

Wind Up Romance 4

Invoked and Kissed 5

Venus 6

Paradox... 7

Refusing Change 8

This Foolish Cockamamie Slam...................................... 9

Arterial Inking 10

The Tide Dances upon Our Toes 11

Flung Back into Flux.. 12

Safari Child.. 13

II. Mother

Mother's Death... 16

Women Are Enormous 18

Arranged Until Gone 20

Alice Gently Folds the Breezing Bubbles 21

Quit Being Such a Baby at the Public Pool..................... 22

Painting the Women at the Elementary School 23

Momma's Garden.. 24

Behind Her Magic 26

I Can Only Blow the Bubbles... 28

III. Struggles

A Poem about Hats... 32

Waiting for This Life 33

MS Me.. 35

I Roast Alone 37

A Woman's Troubles 39

So Close To Your Merrymaking...................................... 41

What Not To Write Your History Professor..................... 44

Entity 46

Where Worlds Collide 48

I Overdose On the Gray Poesy 49

Coveting the Tail 51

IV. The Wife

The "Big One" 54

Is Not Null or [(love)]*[(love)] 55

Spam 57

As If God 58

Stones the Size of His Fist.. 59

I've Been a Bad Girl... 60

I'm Writing a Poem After Dishes 61

I Loved Him Nude.. 63

His Perspective He Is the Island.. 65

I'm Afraid 66

V. Love Gone Astray

Mind over Space.. 70

He Has Horny Growths on His... 72

Desert Relationship 73

Denying Him Sex 74

Sexual Assault 75

So Desperately Is Their Intercourse Part II 77

Spilling From Its Jar... 79

VI. Moods

Fatigue... 82

Full-bodied Laughter.. 83

Her Hostile Oneness 84

Moment of Quietude... 85

Moods.. 86

An Opaque Ritual.. 89

Beyond Insanity... 90

Of Vulgar Images 91

Wandering Furiously Inside 92

In The Length of a Moon-bathing Second 94

VII. Empowerment
Mirror Mirror Rebirth.. 96
From a Slick Sexism.. 97
She Set Herself on Fire.. 99
Summons to Faith... 100
Intensely Me 101
Probably Mistaken For Feminism 102
Jesus Is a Woman.. 103
I Was My First Book 104

I. Nature

Black Secret

We all sat fixed
sunken in a stare

as a white line weaved
in the quiet air.

Thin black arthropod chains
wavered from a black secret

bulb trunk that swarmed
down the twisting filament

and her blades of flaxen hair
a wispy web for the taking

quickly before any onlooker
hysterically warned her.

A hearth for a poisonous abdomen
for the silky cocoon

an uncommon jut
her poised head unaware

until a draft of finger legs
gently kissed her forehead

caressed her cheek then
swiftly buckled under Time.

The Internal Bang of Spring

She has summoned a fling again
in a sweeping plea for another bustle.
In vogue she strikes a tempo

pulsing similar to the stick broom reeds flouncing
into the world clamorously bumping
beating invisible drums of soil whistling.

Blasted ears of autumn leaves diminished in the amplitude
propel each other in their utmost arguments for
symbols that block the on-switch

but she's off on a tangent through simple hidey-holes
whisking inborn tunes strumming
an ambiance of atrocious complaining red tulips.

She puckers up and kisses a blue chorus.
The whole lot of distance has popped.
Holed up in errorless obsession

a pointless dispersal of seed as whimsical disposition
encircles the boisterous mind
into a unique sideshow.

We've all busted earsplitting mad
as she cranks it offensive a whack up
and everything under her fingers dies.

Wind Up Romance

I purfle petal edges, prurient but inaccessible,
flush the kicky from the quicken
beneath splashy bell showers.

Pistachio spindlelegs are poised
as I await the slight tousle of a gent,
an insignificant wistfulness.

To pry, possibly a bloop.

Thorny, saliva dribbling
or of fiddle-faddle fiction, oh please!
My, my, no tangents! Plump capsules
are not to be tentered.

A set tenor rejoices.
Style sways a stigma beyond.
Over the white picket fence
the peal of a resounding propeller blows.

Now remember, talks to windswept moments
blase' is a blotch under the mark.
Just a query dot!
Secretly, a blanc fixe stuttering
is but invisible speck from the spectator.

Not punch trace nor sinewy entry.
Dare it be in gentle arrangement,
excellence of the pistil
then gleam in flip-flop neighborliness.

She sets her shaggy leafage.
He begs the beetles not to gossip,
bends the grass exhausted.

Invoked and Kissed

In stimulated fervid boast
patches of wrangled cumulus
assault a quiet corduroy sky.

Grotesque whimsical bagpipes
of a coarse alto tonal shading
collapse in ludicrous gesture
to liquidate her complexion.

His kiss was a sham,
spontaneity of skillful imitation
to her blindfolded blight.

In do-si-do
on the coattail of a vulgar corsage solar hue,
fingerprints to a filmy coax
invoke an assassin collage
with his odd artillery blatting.

Genuinely saturated along the border
in a conglobe of yielding flattery
she awkwardly bulges forth.

A filigree of lacy petals
clueless thistlelike clusters resisting
and buds in condolences persuade a clump assemblage
under nearby aluminum branches trembling.

She made many feckless attempts
to zipper her prolific naivety
among fragmentary boomy traces
of a peculiar collimation
yet tomorrow she'll bear a downpour.

Venus

Oh what big eyes, so to nectar
I snuggle a fond view, flexible Goddess lines of you.
Beyond spun yarn, I long to kiss.
I swagger among the swallowtails,
tip the viscous fluid of lace, unscathed
as spider yawns my triumph.

Am I pixy cousin you ask
as spittlebug looks on impressed.
A spitting image to the butterfly, I am on the fly.
Beatific wings splay for a sensuous you,
fin treble in savage figment,
my fluttering performance; finesse. I am fly!

If only I could sip from the lip,
wrong wings to heady hair.
Oh Venus, forgive this hauteur.
Entangle me in timid loops of silky dampness,
synchronicity, a fine voice of tick.
And may I say, dear Venus
you are briskly sensitive
as I thaw your hostile attraction
with superior tenure.

Yet, you vibrate as snooty viper
to my desecration!
Have you no mercy?

With weakened pulse, I shiver.
Now a skeletonized lover.
Your liar scrunch is my penitent death,
were only wishes to swim
in your misleading potent allure.

Paradox

Out of her shy cocoon
it must be so laborious
in sync all day long
golden strands of niceties
hair stretching across the dreaming landscape
holding sun up and sun down
around her hot lips
churning earthly content
her murky sea-green eyes half-close
and that upturned nose fights the angle,
the camera snaps a vertical shift of light

when hidden dangers of night
spill through her untouched white breasts.
Chasing day she wears a hat of purple stars
and impish fairies dance
on the last sunbeam
north to south.
Hear her whisper into the gloom.

She's a lullaby, a baby's breath,
a mother's kiss goodnight;
hello to lovers, the wire
disconnects how boredom feels
and affects the mind
pulling her dress connecting twilight.

It must be so exhausting to be summer
and send three months of calendar days
bright skies and puppy love.
There is no one as hardworking and childish.

Refusing Change

Refusing change
the bronzed athlete in sand undresses
with surfing phalanges,
dismisses sophisticated browns and reds

as moist maternal instincts ring
calling him to the hearth.
His windy ear sings.
"But Mother, I cannot

still my heart as a snail slowly creeps
under the cool fringed orchis
nor dream monsoons away in my sleep.
I am merely innocent sport;

a white-tailed jackrabbit
clearing the counselor solstice,
a moonlit meadow inhabit
in an estival of the yellow ponder.

Under a plodding harvest moon
I won't be heavily caught.
My heart is the midsummer noon
in a truelove knot with July."

An oasis broods its piling offensive death.
Ignited, transformed then dull,
his cerebrated breath.
Smoke whistles in a chestnut fall.

This Foolish Cockamamie Slam

Sky capsized under the globe's sweltering rain
forming a torrent of geodesic glower.
It clings to a spot.
An illegitimate keyhole under scraggly pitch pines
is seared in the temperature.

Above the entrance of wild blue lupines are
the keys, Kamer blue butterflies
attaching themselves fluttering;
inland is cracked.

Small branches in a whirlwind crisscross a river
whiffling under the heavens.
Spotted cows lift, and are lost.
My laundry yanks into the vortex unexplained.

A standoffish sun, nothing but a spit of cotton
dabs the fountainhead of lilac drizzle.
We are bamboozled,
the predictable talisman in my pocket and I
that want for a lover.

But it fetches this foolish cockamamie slam!
Spring is nothing more than make-believe; a cruel pity.
So yes my inebriated sailor's lips
are stained in disenchantment forever.

Fools without care quiver.
Petals falsely shiver with precipitation just to slump.
Nonetheless I waltz in stardust bootlace unfastened
obnoxious and full of hips

and my upside-down pineapple cake
with a violet cherry in the core of my soul
is cast beneath my tongue.

It slithers down the throat of time and disappears
in abhorrence of spring's hideous leap
and the sorrow that I dwell in.

Arterial Inking

Fingernail twigs to the wind
slowly "a little to the left please"
touching her barnacle cheek bones.
They turn soft, full and
young and wet.
A sly grin
distorts her bloated hickey lips.
"Down a smidgen."
"Now up a bit."
The indigo flesh of her face swallows
two ballooning eyes with incantations.
"Not so hard."
Stretching her sagging neck she sweats verbs.
Farming the sky is an arduous task;
"quiet now, pierce a little left."
"Up a bit."
She lights late night wicks
breathing vanilla thoughts.
Not yet able to wriggle outside her skin

lusty and tucked beneath the comforter night
she catches a flight inside silver lined dreams,
snaps the wish bone,
sets her wings free.
Her body flattens
and she gives birth to an exhale,
to a wall of fluid afterbirth.
Head spinning, she scribbles a thunderstorm.
"Yes, now!"
"Yes, now!"
"Now!"
"Now!"

Tucking her black legs
around a dirty broomstick
she's absorbed in the downpour
disappearing in a flash.

The Tide Dances upon Our Toes

A warm water cloak;
mildness lurked.
We all sat about the sparkling sand
not knowing what really happened.

A shell of waves fell
dotted the sun-spotted view.
The ghostly breeze lay under,
skin colored foam resting on the ocean floor.

A cold-blooded blanket
of salty spray and breath...
We all sat about the sparkling sand
not knowing what really happened.

One minute they were knee deep
laughing at the surf,
the next minute the sun told a story
as the tide danced upon our toes.

Flung Back into Flux

A peaceful temporary rest
lies before an unsuspecting achromatic winter.
It is artfully pawned to the future.
Spring peacockishly dazzles the daymare
with a rising peachblow press conference
on the whimsical Eastern horizon.

In the breezeway of this slow motion change
belligerent songbird messengers
amplify to an adhesion of raging chimes.
They become a focal point climax.

Like just before the shattering blast
of a booming rocket,
our exhalation is held
tightly within a fist in our lungs.

A bundle of this sugarcoated illusion
stretches with elastic hesitation.
It is in the slingshot exhale
of a colored candy stone
flung back into flux.
Smashed into a thousand pieces
of fluttering beta rhythms
they are bonded upon a bluebonnet landscape.

Safari Child

Things I watch
amidst the pine scented dark
corners of my pointed thoughts
my eye lost in dark pupils;
I cannot scrub
wholly away
the possessive blues.

I gather into the washer
an elephant of woven
colored materials
turn the beetle screw
with a lizard wrench
where once there was a dial
that made it easy

to cock it full. But then I crawl
past the rock
pieces in the kitchen counter tiles. I'm
a safari child circulating
with animals
with dark resources.

The alligator snaps
and the primate
bends its tail, the fowl
preens
from bone to crown. I am king

lion on top of weather;
rain and dust, my cramping haunches
primed, but the head aches
in thoughts of thunder

pushes through
more rain, and I drink and drink
and drink it in, I smoke a blunt
day, tomorrow
it will again

be dry and dark. Yes,
tomorrow melts into dark
until a light emerges
and one of me
dies.

I'll tear flesh.
Rip mirth from it.

I'll eat the sun.
Offer my heart.

The door opens night.
Three children snoring.
A husband snoring.
A common peeve; ordinary life.
I put my child to bed inside a well-kept jungle.

II. Mother

Mother's Death

Oh, glorious wake in rocky meadows
for mother's death
draped in gloomy clouds and dark tears,
rainy day gospel good-byes,
billowy heads are on the other side of pines;
orchards of Pixie Crunch and Sundance bow.

The forest casket
has grown the height of heaven
kindly for eons and
tethered in by splintering mountains
mother lay under a hedge of lilac,

her wrinkled purple veins,
the skin of her swelling tides resurrected
in a shilly-shally hint of illumination
from under the icy dawn
and on...

and on that day

she gave birth to stars,
to full moon threads of gold dust,
downy wings quivering
in streaks of light across my mind
teasing little concealed Milky Way thoughts

and on that day
I marched for her freedom
down on 46th and Lamar St.
Up to a third floor office
I gave my donations and
sang in her spirit.

I gave all her knitted blankets away,
school books, wash tubs, rakes and shovels,
old fashioned kitchen appliances,
a sliver of a rocking chair and two sunken
mattresses that still spring,
clothes for every season, for every size,
and portraits of yesterday's people that I knew well

that were my children
enough to give away with mother gone.

Yesterday's landscapes
where I've never been
all given away

to victims
lost in the shelter of a new day.
And so
we turn another page,
speak of mother no more
draped in gloomy clouds and dark tears,
downy wings quivering

streaks of reflection across my mind
teasing little concealed Milky Way thoughts,
and on that day
I marched for her freedom
down on 46th and Lamar St.

to a safe home; support for
survivors of domestic violence.

Women Are Enormous

He tried to skillfully close
the night on her mysterious dark cavern
sliding his fingers
past the mouth of mankind
to free the light.

Trapped in the black hole,
star-shaped clusters of a thousand blooms
hid from daylight all summer long
to be plucked by his hand tool.

On creative impulse
he pulled the purple shades,
painted the walls with smoothness
and upon the dark polished stone he sculpted the round Venus;
her pubic triangle and enormous breasts
and her middle body bulging with pregnancy.

Executing a choir of grass
she laid the door of tree rings aside
celebrated inside the shape
of a solid twenty-thousand years.
The neighborhood trees
bent to the nimbus encircling her head:
a volume of clay illusions.

One thing at least is clear; he tried
to skillfully close the night on her mysterious dark cavern,
simple shells joining her neck
to her painted torso and engraved bulbous thighs.
He slid his fingers past
the poisonous mouth of mankind

up her tower-flanked stairway
to her streaming consciousness
yet his horned helmet impaled the unleashed landscape
and he never plucked the treasured pebble
in the form of a face

so she remains an abstract
image called art
without even a hundred historians or lovers
debating the rage of timeless passion;
the inescapable entity
that fell from the horizontal heavens.

Arranged Until Gone

We arranged the shapes,
my five year old and I.
She at the beginning of her elementary pages
through points to triangles
while I regularly left the comfortable circle.

As for triangles that fit into square boxed lines,
we needed two to make a square.

She counted sides of rectangles,
two long and two short.
My shortened thoughts fit neatly into
a small square that started in a simple circle
then elongated as time went on.

Labeling the figures, we both colored them.
Corners, sides, sorting, counting until organized
I enjoyed the colored figures more and more
just as she did learning them.
Little of me was seen then.
Some could say they were going blind
when they couldn't see me well.

I even wanted the colors to fit with the shapes.
Each day patterns were made and felt just the same.
My image was disappearing as I worked.

We arranged the boxes; squares to rest inside each other
starting with the smallest and ending with a great big box.
'Mommy this is fun', she would say.

She at the beginning of her elementary pages,
and I perfecting my rearranging for all to see
for a lifetime as I disappeared.

Alice Gently Folds the Breezing Bubbles

The damage from the nuclear monster
is almost streak-free,
irreversible sweet plus sour
from skin to bone
even though it stays in our fading yellow
faces an almost blue sky gravy.
In peppered temperature the sugar hophead
nibbles away blackberry skin ourselves
covered with lucky charmed red and green and purple
marshmallow surprise eyes puffing cocoa night
flaking frosted bowed heads purely
in need of a miracle.

Mickey Mouse and Donald Duck go squeaking
go quaking, they go!
Super Mario Brothers on their tail running
for their lives a turmoil
a noodged muddy stew.

Apologizing too many flavors confused
in the hodgepodge,
our positively charged dreams in thin layers
just under a dappling tide disease.

And Winnie-the-Pooh reaches for his honey jar
rising on the foaming lip, up, up oh bother!
Alice gently folds
the breezing bubbles into her pocket
back to Wonderland where it's safe.

Oh yes, unlike each other sorry
quivering wishes upon one billion stars
"I wish you'd have left me and my children alone"
to wear soft white cotton
to finger-paint the clouds one at a time
one simple color each drifting by.

Quit Being Such a Baby at the Public Pool

The public pool is for waders, splashing jumpers
for feet that tap the bottom in weightless tag,
for underwater red-eyed dreamers
and shy dippers that gossip minutes to the towel.

On the diving board after two children jumped,
peering from the height; the chlorine blues beckoned.
My dirty diving will be disposable beneath,
so is anyone watching I thought.
I walk the plank feeling grotesque
and wither in a breeze.
Eight strung out toes point to the sky, two little ones tuck under.
Toe nails pray portending to catch my shivering eye.

In dizzy remembrance when this was a nonstop game of youth;
I'd climb the fluctuating ladder, run the board
and in perfect form greet the watery crested plane with a smile.

In a full gasp and teetering tip toe plunge
(intimate now with my fear in mid air)
I overextend myself, bottom heavy, and I slap the hard surface.
Hands went first, head second, chest
and then unfortunately my swinging torso.
My back burned as I chased thoughts
around the painful embarrassment of my spectacle.

I left my expertise gumption twenty years back
at the Hawthorne Pool
with silly light-weight ten year olds,
with hearts that pumped natural energy
that could power all of Los Angeles County *and* its neighboring towns.

Yes, back with my youth...my back!
I asked the kids, "Is my back red?"
They didn't even notice. They shrugged my aching skin off
as nothing more than "oh Mom, quit being such a baby!"

Painting the Women at the Elementary School

The droopiest obesity splatters
flumped gossip against
my ear,
fatty feline emotions.
I need a drop cloth
to catch their autumn colors
dripping here in the spring.
A spill of discontentment
ready to hide under the earth
is the forgotten body of women,
their bones stiff, leafless
a smug trunk without floweriness.

If I had my druthers,
understanding their depleted
pastels, lack of vibrant splashes
I would brush their limbs
in a flip-flop
of adaptable heirlooms;
the velvety purple, 'Cardinal de Richieu"
globular lemon-yellow, 'Marie Van Houtte'
or smear pale pink, 'Old Blush' into their cheeks
and feathered hair a field
of Canada lilies, and painted Virginia bluebell dresses.

Within one week of my big brush makeover
the shades would be noticeable;
instead of a Mona Lisa sneer
laminated on a hard wood face split personality
they'd portray their plump unfurling lips
in honest upward creases
at the lush floral corners.

Momma's Garden

to love or not to love your Momma
so early in the morning
rifle in hand
cursing like a banshee
anyone help that woman?
that rebel without a cause
to kill the drum
the drum inside our ears

who on earth
would cultivate issues with this woman?
when what's left of her senses
has been tossed
to ignite a spark of terror in the next
perverted piper
calling us to our death over the cliffs
instead of life saving renewal
creeping nearer our death so she can stroke us
with her hunger for distance

wailing death
a death in soundness
judgement tucked in neat little balls of disgust
pressed with divided attention to the angst
into ears as we walk away
surprised

did we see and hear what was really going on?
or were we the cursed for having come near?

and we drop one by one
our original mentality
flaking over what might have been a good day
she is no dried up prune
in saucy winter's forward motion
unyielding beyond the white picket fence

our ashes are sprinkled
blown of carbon uprising
predicted in her wailing
Mother sympathetic earth
from the swollen vibrations
against our tender surface
labor rising to the sky

Behind Her Magic

She has been slipping
into brilliant perennial breaths
vining the peppermint striped straw.
Ringing in her bellflower ears

are peachy whispers parading
between her wide eye-like spots
on fuzzy skinned pink to yellow
corn silk hair the length of heartleaf cheeks.

In her blanket flower dress
a daisy bloom is dwarfed
in an old garden sit.
Up, up fertile glances

above the table sky
are round see-through blush-white
pretty maids in Mary's rows
and Cinderella's silver bells

where "everything is hotsy-totsy!"
Look up, up milky chocolate breezing down,
petals form perfect globes
a baby's breath of candytuft

button-shaped chrysanthemums,
pompoms and poppies with pixy dust.
She drifts mesmerized in a river bend
knit of sugar and spice

dots of inflorescence,
curved indentations glazing the air
spurting her giggling sight.

Swallows of flossy polka dots
are finished in liquid glass Peter Pan style.
She sets the peppermint striped straw aside,
tosses silver jacks,
bounces a green rubber ball.
A brimful of poring zest
lies behind her magic pose for my instamatic
in a polished Hush My Dolly pout.

I Can Only Blow the Bubbles

In my sleepy abstinence the door is crashed!
With a taste of berry dessert
I pop the standard issued pink pill mole
in case of spilling top secrets
then I swim in an untrustworthy sugar fix.
There are cherry visions rolling
from whipped cream
on hot fudge sundaes at Farrell's Ice Cream Parlor.
They cry "she's a pig!"
I'm pinned.

Below my hoisted chair
in ceremonious hubble-bubble
my bib falls to a melting checkered linoleum
into a hollow iridescent globe.
The Radio Flyers given my firstborn and second born
float by.
Wings from my youngest
surreally flap in delusional intrigue.

This effervesce marks a lively buoy dream
yet it negotiates ovum madness.
I find myself upside-down firmly glued
conforming to an easy chair.
It's a parade!
Smiles for everyone.
Moms with their children at Lawrence Whelk's
sing tiny bubbles,
tiny bubbles.
The bleachers kiss my four-year-old bloomers
and Walt Disney fantasizes
about transparent pink elephants popping.

The picture tube merrily in black and white
blinks movies of chubby women, waddling schemes
in two-tone happy face smocks.
Their angry Russian faces paint me in a pie as a blackbird.

I'd speak but I can only blow
bubbles off the top of Vin Diesel's bald head
clutching his tattooed biceps,
and blow the bubbles from my standard issued S-X4 gun.
Staring into Vin's eyes that turn into parachutes
and poof us out of the pie
I find myself slow dancing in the Bahamas with a wigged out guy named
Hugo
as I awaken to my kids fighting over the television shows.

III. Struggles

A Poem about Hats

It is difficult to write
a poem about hats.
I will write about the way a mind
sits nicely on the head.
I have been
fitting

comfortably into my own space lately.
Although
I am wary
that a contradictory hand, a
grotesquely pernicious hand
might lift my mind off.
This is the time for October's

frights and ghouls followed by
thanks and giving, and more thanks and
giving and the big squeal of a new baby year.
A hundred and one

cotton balls snug
inside a jar; lid gently closed.
A door that clicks shut, quietly.
A tootsie roll unraveled.
A pool without a dive.
The new Easter dress;
no stains, no tear, no wear. Nowhere.
Things to do and not doing them.

Fresh linen.
Unwrinkled skin.
The way a calm mind
harmoniously sits on the tame head.
No gasping,
no shuttering,
no shock,
and the breath of the dishes and laundry still stack.

Waiting for This Life

If I had been there
slipping into the slick gas station
thirty minutes earlier
I would be sprouting into my next life

perfectly balancing the perforation
of a metal ball like a seed bullet
with suspenders of bloody leaves holding
this ignored fleshy papier-mâché'

swirling blue and gold vase of my neck.
Impregnated with the suicide of thought
I'd be crushed alive
inside the force of a luscious rose garden;

hovering a foot above
wearing my stunned guardian angel as a hat,
innocent feather-brained wings sprawled,
covering my hotbed primordial cranium.

If I turn out to be crushed by despair
warming with dark caps in a mumbling kitchen
warned but without real cause for any disaster,
a superstitious black cat crosses my path

and you see weird TV specials about
how in death the soul is a
light streaming from
the corpse;

something visible or tangible
from the other side, or an unexplained
pang I sometimes have
caused by ill intent or voodoo pins,

even karma circles things alive
into positive electric change. But certainly
* "when you try to change any single thing,
you find it hitched to everything else in
the universe." My spirit could know this.
But why am I hearing a rat-a-tat-tat
ominous echo, invisible to this nude orb?
Is my timing gingerly off?

If the clock has stopped somewhere from its fastidious
transformation, to tick

a ghoulish direful luck
would be

some earthbound farce;
spontaneously loathsome and bushy-tailed
with claws cutting
the other side allowing impassable fiends

to fog my senses like a filmy vapor
that sticks to one's vacuous thoughts,
especially when that greasy *damn-it-all*
had finally reached a peak of relaxation.

What kind of bareheaded destruction
could this impish
out-of-body-dementia be?
Waiting for this life

to be what it is not yet?
I do know this;
those innocent
feathered-brained wings are of positive spirit.
I wear my guardian angel as a hat.

* "when you try to change any single thing,
you find it hitched to everything else in the universe."
John Muir

MS Me

MS me, twist of genetics
waiting for the shut down
the hobbling, the gasping
and knees buckling
as if anyone knew why
as if anyone cared

how precious my breath is
longing to be set
free, nerves lining the Universe along
a spinal chord of mayhem.

Dangerous jazz, blues
of the brain, we can see
the far island of loss and gain
a thousand miles just searching to rest.
Danger captain!
Please take me in your arms,
I can no longer fight

and smooth the windy ends of every
frazzled beginning.
Endings, every day shuffling this deck
with broken fingers sailing the sky.

I'll stash the card up my sleeve
in hopes
I can play it every tricky day
and I'll ice another birthday cake
with a steady hand.
Make ready my way
because
I am coming home perfect.

Parts of me that have been, nevertheless
parts of me disassociated; all
hardened love.
I'll stay together a dynamo I will.
Together
jerking myself together
because
I am coming home perfect
bruises and all.

I Roast Alone

Eleven snakes swerve as thoughts, in, out
between threads of my hairy-head jungle.
Oils along my scalp fuel self-ignition.
Fire is freaking brilliant.

I refuse to leave my home
because there are creatures stirring my soul
and a sort of fear runs wild.

Sometimes I weep into the pane
behind broad dapple green leaves,
a basket weave, a two-tone camouflage.
I pace unsteady
to this skull drum thumping
from heart to embers.

So I find one cigarette.
Into the empty cupboards I crawl.
It's there.

Smoking today is not like yesterday.
My scars have almost mended.
The scabs inside of forefinger and middle
I've picked for hobby.

This place will not go down.
Chase the tiger from this dwelling, I dare you.
I'll smoke this last cigarette in bed.
The mattress, the brush, sheets, and my fingers won't
go; they won't burn again.

There are no distress calls, no smoke signals.
SOS. (There's a thought.) The last time
I scrawled those three earsplitting gory letters;
well let's reiterate: "I won't burn again."

No mirrors.
No Morse code.
I'm alone plucking each hair, each tiny morsel from
(my hairy-head jungle) to feed this twisted thrill.
Over it, I roast alone. Sirens sing. They never find me.
Jungle beasts copulate on the edge with the damned.

But I am with me, familiar and unconcerned.

A Woman's Troubles

Get rid of
the rock in my forehead,
rid of the stick in my neck
thrust halfway between
my right shoulder blade and left and
up my brain stem.

Holy petals, I pick the top of my curls and
I love me and
I'm not intoxicated
like a starving rose that can't find sunlight.
I just love me.

So those who speak
of me
so vague in their minds,
your hearts will swallow crow
and all its dark feathers, its bleak beak
with the esoteric
language
of your own bondage.

I love me.

Chaos roots itself, roots itself
rooting itself into roads with potholes filling up
with rainwater and $300,000.00 homes,
rushing into manmade lakes
with fake rocks and sticks and stones
and as I drive down State Line
I find only one
farm house left
surrounded by bulldozers and wet earth.

Muddy water can break this
concrete pelvis that
sits deep in the thought of this established aching
like a new tract home
or a condominium.
It can be
carried away by the flood
and it won't let my
feet shuffle past the rising puddles into spring.
The jinni seed
that seeped into one of my ears a long time ago
like a ghost whispering obscenities or affections
I have to ink past
its duel embraces, these
pent up images like a smothering mudslide
as if I spit on my own white memory
of the Big House and its mother-of-pearl gates

and something volatile
caught fire
on a red hot sentence
leaking from the gas tank
trailing my conundrum montage mind.

But I still remember
when he kicks the door in
there will be a fatality and
nothing but a baby evil born;
another storm, its goggling eyes,
mascara running down
its cheeks, madly burned
hair and raggedy cotton
second hand clothes
and another, and another storm

whether I have confidence
that the sun will shine or not;
I fancy liberation.

So Close To Your Merrymaking

It was the light I remember.
You won't let me forget.
Your white truck bounced off pot holes
like a punk band in the silence of a praying church.
Two-by-fours banging.
A red burning light behind the wheel.
Your eyes black holes.

What a fascination steering
that beat up old thing going twenty
and one-hundred-and-twenty
at the same time unglued.

You were lightning?
Sitting alone with the airy fairy
dust from the chemical lab firing your
mind to pieces; what you needed
when you traveled so far
while sitting still on the hill.

What does your white truck need
so it won't clunk-chink?
Cool water for the engine?
You might have pricked its nerves.
Only dry dunes and rotten teeth out there.

It has to drive you. To go fast.
I saw you there. Do you still
want my positive stimulus
so close to your merrymaking?
You couldn't possibly like my road.
I don't even bubble over like I used to.

The tension on Mountain Road
just below the Dam that night
in a crowd of speed
freaked three or four heads into one

soup under the hood.
All in you.
Will you roll over?
Don't flood with entities.

We'll come to terms;

that grinding gladsome heart beat. Right?
It sputters.
Your butt slides back and forth along
the drivers seat and you lurch forward
as if to help it.
I'm ambushed with your

erect chink, a satisfaction choking off.
Does it help to topple my certainty?
I don't like racing you know.
You falter too close to me frazzled.
And your mobile always needs a tank full.
I think the biggest win
was when you asked me
are you scared of my truck?"

It runs oblique.
It's loud.
It's violent.
"Some bits of my spine are still in the treads," I answer.

But you don't surprise me one bit.
I've seen you a dozen times before.
I've seen your stupid son too
in his red rocket.
He was cutting the moon in half.

Both your faces submerged in
icy elation
breaking tiny blood vessels
dripping down warm
toxic mares.

I awakened to you climbing on,
something about
the scent of you, like an old man that doesn't shower,
like burning skin or rotten cheese.

Your mind jangled above my head.
Your face tightly pinned to your ears.
Your hair fell out leaving a trail.
Your white murmuring truck left without you.

The door slipped.
My legs jittery.
Cigar smoke pricked my nose.

"There goes your white truck."
"Can you go now?"
"No!"
"Can you go anyway?"
Flattened tires,
it speeds down the center line.
Hot holy rubber! The rims are bent on vacation.

What Not To Write Your History Professor

I'm sorry I have every right
to miss class today, this flight
my psychological rift; I will
explain

as I have coughed into an entire box of soft tissue
green mucous, milked the syrup
bottle out of every sweet drop of Phenergan codeine,
a whole bottle of Doxycycline four times a day...
am I going on?

I feel sorry for myself.
Tylenol doesn't help.
The pills that mother gives me...
Why did Jefferson Airplane change their
name to Jefferson Starship? I used

to live under the runways
for twenty-three years; did you know
I can yell twice as loud as a 747?
The airplanes take off thrice as much at night as day

the decimal levels almost
the volume of a rock concert.
I am a mother of four;
my husband,
my oldest
my second oldest
and my youngest.
I have taken seventeen hundred milligrams
of decongestant.

Is it the first day I am missing?
No! I am staring
cautiously palpitating
heaving
the delirium night
probably without a sinus infection at all
wishing the days would make love
all day
all night
passing time
waiting for the late show...
my world art definitions are a tad bit

incomplete but if I crawl to the library
when I am without
aphrodisiacal remedy
or melody of desire in mind
I might be able to catch a volume
of encyclopedia.

I will be better in my
weekly best...
graduating
transferring
please don't drop me...
sincerely,
me, you know me
such a short distance to the college
steps to your class eternally in Stonehenge.

Entity

fierce entity
the toddler nimbly attaches himself
to the doll house window, pries at the slick pane
his vain efforts
bang

crash against empty glass
sparkling buckets full of saline rain
clank-clink
forced suddenly
from the dark cloud
above his curly locks

(his sister's pink doll house rocks)

and I am snug in a bent fetal
eminent domain of dream
while a squatting baby pounds
screeches outside
in battle

where
the young child twists his spherical
retinas orbiting a skull-bursting sky
eyelashes, vicious limbs
batting to catch a glimpse
of me snoring past
every spoiled
dirtied
positively charged
toddler hostilities he gets away with...

starts so young
a behavior...

and to think
his little sister who arranged me there;
plastic
properly retired in limbo
she laughs at my plumy lips
my head soft on plastic feathers
his sister who put me there

will call tomorrow's mother
to pick her brother up
to dab every shade of gray
and offer him a peace of giant cookie
a milky white cloud-nap
a kiss

smiling
confiscating the doll house
mother kisses sister

winks "top secret"
sets her house high
on the sunlit desk;
there's no breaking in
no more pouring down
drowning rage

Where Worlds Collide

Springs of light-dawn
nourish the evidence of their visit.
A fork to the wrist vine,
drops of red wine,
mineral-rich blood-raspberry
clusters have drawn
an influx of the nocturnal
staining windows with a red-out barren moon
where worlds collide
in timeless disharmony.

Nature's thirsty violence
can't cut the bloody beast
with knives, sticky black-red ooze
on their parasitic lips,
licks of the lava rose
smooth glistening bare necked vine
two "bite me" holes

and nothing is left but a parched Venus,
salt-skins-and-dust,
scent of coyotes on the breeze,
spilled toxic liquids befitting a quackery
each hour, every hour once sipped

the need to apprehend the meaning of
an attractive *manipulation to be stripped.*
Rawboned over the door frame
leaves of white veins
laid to rest just missing

Cupid naked in the window
stuck with his own arrow,
above him garlic hanging differently
to deliver the velvet encroachment from sin.

I Overdose On the Gray Poesy

I overdose on the gray poesy
in its marvel
and gustiness between emergencies.
I swim submitting to depths
telling them
telling all of them
it was a poetic vice that failed me.

Why would anyone talk to me
behind my back
behind my consciousness?
From an idiot stagnation
I arose to die.
On the page

as if it were heaven
my cognition lost itself in imaginary people
and I asked them
"do you need my life?"

All the gossiping soul had to offer;
the gray poesy whispered backwards
so I couldn't quite understand it.

So I ate it backwards from the gut out.
It was my trip around counter clockwise
that I am guilty of, I
told authorities and leaders of the
suicide that led to

dreams of poetry. Actually it told nothing different but it felt.
They proposed everyone die
in the written word.
Called it remedy.
Each single page of day
a serious person should
gorge.
Breathe the pristine white in
you are born again blow
into an invisible balloon then let it go.

Watch it rocket, spit, curl
into the air into its plastic
being and then
air;

Sylvia and Anne
get off your pity pot in sky.
Relax in death.
It is fine.
We reek of your
clandestine affair with the written word.
Its entrails haunt us.
"Inadmissible in the room of life,
dauntingly all that life thrust under the tongue"
I
can

wave a white flag
cover it in a checker board of sentences;
"dying is an art I guess."
Whether we do it well or not.
My chest will fall punished

into my spine tonight and I will be alone.
The season between seasons I am guilty
of being alone.
Or desire life-gloom.
I can't

console this farthing life.
Renewed from its gnashing death.
And there it is again
another

gray poesy
in its marvel
and gustiness between emergencies.

(Inspired by Sylvia Plath and Anne Sexton)

Coveting the Tail

The investigation has gone on
since the beginning of mankind,
three decades for a woman not unlike me
who evidently covets the man's front-sided *tail*;
it swishes she's jealous,
it protrudes she's unhappy,
it slices the bleak terrain creating rainbows,
angelic song, a life-size lance saving the world
promising air we inhale,
a smooth-pointed *tail*
to fill sunken features or clear a space
in women's indecision, it's nature to
settle disputes; she's sad, the organ can
stretch from one side of the earth to the other
similar to laying one's cloak down
for the woman to walk on water, the man's *tail,*
a jawless lover kisses the night tranquil,
the *tail* runs and swims, it can move
gently horizontal
or vertical or invert, the front-sided *tail*
slaps the common fly from the soup
significant and historic, the organ
the tail tills the soil composing parallel lines
to drop seeds while the woman is fatigued
jealous, languishing: the woman takes her flashlight
for a closer look in a lapse of grace
she envelops its nature
and with a magnifying glass to witness
its brilliance
in an outburst she cries "where is it?"
She had been wishing to have one, to be one
to be the out-and-out extremity,
to play the instrument
to become the legendary tool, yet all
she can do is covet and emphasize neatness
and sorting amidst her chaotic shadowing
of an ailing frame of mind:
"Oh my the tail! Oh my the tail!"

IV. The Wife

The "Big One"

The upside-down lovers
slow dance in spontaneous optimism,
gentle stretches of elasticity for hours
within a topsy-turvy marathon world.

The top of their heads swirl
in a centered sky, the "big one"
a rock python as slithering earth
round and round
gyrates against their aching feet;
its jaws clamped onto its own tail
like a wheel.

Snakes respond to bumping vibrations
so the key to the firmly twisted lovers
to stay in the marathon
is to smoothly swish their feet,
gently breathe the sky
as the snake squeezes
and rolls in a circle.

They silently love the heavy-bodied
contracting sunup to midnight,
they dare not antagonize
by speeding their hip to hip steps
nor lose their balance
and collapse with exhaustion
for fear "the big one"
will lose interest in its own tail.

When the night
equals a chilling ten degrees
the "big one" unravels,
tosses the lovers into the air
then slinks back into its dark hole.

Is Not Null or [(love)]*[(love)]

The fertile earth
is a loosely fastened database.
I'm erratically searching her fiction
using wildcards as a last chance,
as a necessary strange compromise.
Abnormally high
feverish questions arise.

Are you the one who turns
your reader-only attribute off
in a festivity of prolific fervor?
Do you allow changes of garland to loop
between two points?
Or will your file become spine curved,
head bowed
rocking,
arms and legs against chest?"

I'll press buttons
on the switchboard of indefinite small numbers
of biological reproduction
and navigate your premarital form
into my report, select a query
of exceptional values
and then postulate your unique design view.

The wizard is an accurate prescience.
An omen of sorting
names A through Z and still
the primary key remains the same
field seizing advance of love.

We can start with a blank database.
Then linked preorbital forms with buttons
should create an impression, an initial spark.
I'll press your button affectionately.

And you mine.
Our unreasonably obsessive
need for a visual requires
a fetching OLE, a bitmap
of two lovers kissing
embedded where we join.
The wildcard, a criteria
will be IS NOT NULL, and if that
isn't enough, [(love)]*[(love)].
No default.
The perfect match.

Spam

Put on your night jacket.
You're going to find the chill.
I'll unravel a flailing sensibility against your Spam neck.

I twist the key and roll
the tin belly,
into squeaky joints.
So tighten that cinch, tie
and slip on
your greasy house shoes.

I roll your tin skin.
I roll it coiled beneath your feet
and savor your fatty pockets,
bits of gristle within your meat,
lick the salty tongue,
pluck your eyeball and suck it clean.

After I've uncontaminated your eyeball
from the overwrought drama that you've seen
I'll pop it back in,
back in the socket
tenderly so you can see yourself, clearly
naked.

As If God

Reaching
as if God
were somewhere under the first layer
of my skin tone
and might have been folded lightly
maybe even ironed and pressed delicately
into small helpless rectangles, anyway,

and I a porous heaven
displayed powdery sheets tucked,
unfolded thighs,
this whole heart
a pillow for his thinking.

His body lay closed in a fetal position
on the white surface of an Edenous garden
then as if just to
quietly breathe
he stretched before my wet yin his dry yang
newborn hooks into me clawing
at the light, I kicked
open from the heat with a flood and I almost cooed
before I realized
we were cultivated flowers
and I had fallen
from my pot.

Stones the Size of His Fist

I have a foot length coat with pockets
that hold stones the size of his fist
twenty or thirty at a time.
A hat I've had for fourteen years
to bite back the wind.
My heavy hiking boots did time.

The stream gets deep.
Life enjoys that depth.
A black and white photo
I know just after a snowstorm;
the picture isn't balanced.

I know white.
Yes, I know.
Everyone knows on white.
The letter I leave behind,
my mind in ink.

Feet like cement.
Wet rope burning sadness
I kiss the fluid edge.
Winter waits for me to look still
from under glass.

I've Been a Bad Girl

I thought I'd lost my appetite, but
I've been a bad girl.
The leading contestant, a wordy winner
easily leaves my better half.

I thought I talked myself out of,
and showed sound judgment
but the rushing
the blinking
the whitewashed icing
the defeating threats inside

the flashy craving
enchantress;
my eyewitness desire to set things right;

a lubricious red-blooded lust.
Every crumb worth licking
and then an
immediate high.

Poor flimsy better half;
reserved
and inhuman.

I'm Writing a Poem After Dishes

I'm writing a poem after dishes
have written the suds. The scum talked
for half an hour, never
heard that before.
It whispered
insane.
Write.

I tell you the hard joy
is not coming out
of the mind.
The hard thing
is the same old
scrub brush

the old wrinkled thing
a century of filth
that sours the thought
of a wild embellishment

having never experienced
the beauty
whatnot of never experiencing.
To me, to me, to the reader
who

should leave it all alone;
my expression climbs down
this minuscule existence
that hangs on a ventricle and beats

until it is pulped.
It isn't fiction. It is real.
Real is the headache.
Real is the coffee,
the cold toilet seat.
Real isn't the person who
enjoys telling tales
bursting bubbles with sinister
remedies of revenge
that twist the heart
so it won't comply with a single word

imagined or not

to leave the word alone;
a crying infant
wanting to suckle my fingers
tapped
onto the mind's desire

and leave it alone on the page for someone else
to contemplate
a bottle of thought
to calm the insignificance
of this written poem

a poem

that expresses itself every day
locked up without knowing
how.

I Loved Him Nude

The earth is no cadaver
though the land will be dissected.

Frozen inside; stuffing, raging, slipping,
I crack without leveling.

I burn in the quaking night.
I shake.

Into ridges I tremble
then vibrate greedily along plateaus.

Out of my velvety torment rumbling
he comes desiring me.

Straddling my dwelling
I have waited too long for love

and I shrink to the Universe embarrassed.
I am no more myself.

Rocking the base descending
I find my skin fueled by lust and clay molds.

I love him nude so much it hurts
the center of my earth.

Our thundering friction;
we are soiled.

Shifted.
Unbridled eagerness from dust

crashing into cemented valleys
quite awkward

we hope it never ends.
Catching our breath

we implore nature's curve;
"take time and spare us"

as we blow sand from our limbs
and climb from the wreckage.

His Perspective He Is the Island

She is two hundred pounds of water,
fleshy blue and creatures within.
I harden at her touch
create the eye to eye contact watching her
bat lashes with charming avoidance,
slow without moving facial muscles
calm within her I rise.

I waddle inside her depths.
She hugs me down.
Her layers envelope my thick trunk
and I spring a leak
but interact as if consistent
as if in awe
I bob in the surf of it
sure fire to use what's left
fondle and kiss to make up
for what I know she can't feel.

Tomorrow she'll be off somewhere
tramping around under
an indigo hurrah and become swallowed
no doubt by her own desire to mold
these pointed edges so strong
that her fingertips meekly fall
with every thrust and wiggle.

I'm Afraid

I'm afraid for what I've done
that I haven't done
when the strike comes against me by you
or by him or they and my withstanding
standing unmoved unvoiced and killed me off
or I ran wild away.
What the celebration of love
should have brought...

Haven't I done enough to you?
Haven't you done enough to me?
Those who know zilch
who sense I've done something to them,
that too I experience
although what I've done originated in them;
you to me to you,
what we've done to each other.
I'd rather have flowers and lies
for this coffin of life lowered deep in my

sorrow for all of us who remain
connected somehow
(somehow rejected and attracted)
at the same time dying.
It forgives me for the origin for my life;
having done these things to all of you.

I'm sorry I'm not a man
to forgive the seed you settled in me
that rises up the same as
you and I
just like we two
they are so much that I reject

what anybody has done or not done.
Some seeds from those who
celebrated as if love were an accident
laughed at me as I got their seed cut out of me.
I'm afraid for what I've done that I haven't done
when the strike comes against me.

The true sin is when I tell the truth;
what we've all done to each other and nobody else bones up
as their bodies turn to ash.
What else can I give my children who I've born
into what we've done but that.

V. Love Gone Astray

Mind over Space

Everyone always spoke about how it enlarged to twelve
or fifteen inches long, but I was alone with it and
its murmuring, and I knew it had a mind of its own

but it was surrounded by two-by-fours
and metal pieces that kept it sturdy,
and nails and sheet rock and plaster

or whatever it is that keeps some things
so vague and so upright.
There could have been an army to help it

hold its own atoms rising going nowhere
completely hidden, or anonymously spouting orders
but completely part of the whole regime

towering over me like a ceiling or the firmament,
yet it had a sort of nothingness at times
that made me want to look inside and

reach my hand and search for treasures.
Other times I wanted to spray it for bugs when
legs wiggled out of a crack in it because sometimes

I felt if the fracture grew too large, I'd have to glue its gap.
No matter if it was an important and
integral part of keeping things together or not

it was purposely put there by its builder.
Still I was forced to let it alone most times, that's how
I knew the fortifications wouldn't tumble down

just for the very overemphasized space it took
which most times I believe was an exaggeration.
But once when somebody accidentally

punched the wall, I could see through, I could
steal a look from end to end inside the hole, and then
I knew for sure that it was only around one inch long
by two inches at the most, and I wasn't
really concerned about whether the house
could breathe or not, but why everybody

spoke about how it's a great deal larger and much
more vital than it really is.
Who's fooling who here anyway?

He Has Horny Growths on His...

He has horny growths on his
toes; corns, roots I think he said. I could
plant his feet in the back yard, his
elastic torso won't be forgotten;

he might, (surprisingly), expel blossoms next spring
if I water him faithfully, then again he might
swank god awful weeds, or he might
shrivel under a blistering solar hue,
in his gory hell he might even cultivate
a hymen that I would pluck for my vase
or simply hydrate with the morning dew
just to sizzle in bitter wonder

or I could bury his feet
in a pot on the sill
near the western window
as he patiently awaited
my weathered hand
to spill him a trickle of hypnotic liquid
or open the shades to the hysterical moon.

But I'd never have to hear his screw this screw that.
I'd cover his head
with a bandanna in the frigid winter
or any time he viciously sneezed.

Desert Relationship

His lyric touch
sang beneath
her lace-like webbing,
a smooth cultured pearl
feeling a bright desert star would emerge

he smoothed
over the still mesh
with sandpaper hands
stiff-legged, he rubbed
in a virile frenzy
opened her delicate orchid petals

rounding off corners that didn't belong
that seemed to be
the knotted black widow night.
Darkly, maraschino cherry colored

she was cunningly unmissed.
A creation from sand dunes
fluttered away as a butterfly
off the edge of her lip
not a whisper.

She merely clasped her mercurial
disposition with an indifferent
visual solution, finely feminine, without
a wonder
a stream of consciousness under the desert floor;
shadowy, sour, grape-colored.

He gave the morgue sun
his morning-gift
his stake
dried up fish bones, pitiless

Death Valley at midday;
ravens picked his cotton flesh.

Denying Him Sex

I have no lips
to revive the dead corpse
cracked glass eyes
evidence to shallow visions
every pore oozing a surly
incomplete life tilted
decomposing cursively profane
like the curl of the small g
loveless flesh, God's silent vengeance
shading the sharp edge
incised charming glassware
with long snaking S's

the cuss, long live the cuss
rudely decorating
melting into one's own horizon
no lovely wine can fill
nor soft touch befalls the want
calling evil on bent knee
for voluptuous curves to the pointed end
and the cushy skin unhardened

short, thick tooth
from the sauce of dancing injury
respectfully lowered
into the realms of darkness
loveless flesh, God's silent vengeance
there is no denial
in no thank-you
S's into the curl of g
worming his twelve foot deep skull
I have no lips
to revive the dead corpse

Sexual Assault

At Safehome
she comes out
of the closet, at first a trickle
she hears her attacker
somewhere outside the steamy window
somewhere in the snow covered hills
like the sound of a dump truck
and crashing cans, her face gets
as red as the little roses
in rows across her breast
between buttons,

unbuttoned she screamed "no"
you're hurting me
and his mockery, his boot against
the door jamming
her into the corner
but her blood slithered over his boot
up his leg against gravity
like when Buddha set the bowl in the stream
and it flowed upstream against
the current.

She speaks at the Safehome
getting redder, like a pressure cooker
she speaks quicker

up his thighs and groin
her blood travels
covering his chest
beating in his heart her fear
covers his face
a gushing river pushing
the door open
like a sign, like a prophet speaking
of what's to come.
He still walks
in denial
covered in the color of a rose

lined up at attention on her blouse
some between the buttons
fall to her feet
no trace of resolve
on her face.
Roses are in her heavy steps
but her blouse is white.

So Desperately Is Their Intercourse Part II

She sees the coming of things that haven't changed
just as they have
looked through the windows
at her naked useless conversations.

So "lend an ear" they say. It's a giant
listening, moving its blind eye
filling up her home
smashing the walls.

Inside somebody's home
is a crazy legend
of extraordinary power;
recorded distance
never having to meet
the person anybody hates.

Memories of privacy stolen,
peace of mind
blink, blink, an unusually large
hand squeezes
the fifth day Friday.
The shrugged off conscience
reeks of what nobody has
said or done;

nobody has done anything
to "beat that wild woman."
Again
overlapping days
in the mist of anybody's home
that nobody has met crying.
Soon there will be no love
to fix the sky

or a fix to set their giant free
so desperately is their intercourse
of antipathy
knowing nothing of any woman
or any wife
or any children's perseverance
under the rainbow
that nobody has seen.

Spilling From Its Jar

the ink spurts a chill
up and down a paper spine
up and down, and down and up your mind
it blots out the taste of old root
of dead meat and tasteless vine

dabbled on the grit of intent
moral less intentions reek of habit
a splotch inside the eye
of invaluable cunning
smudged murky to the temples

carbon pigment in your heart
and coiled around it soot of lies
ink as black as souls that burn
burnt and grilled on excessive you
the ink spurts a chill
up and down a scene of trickery

just Arial type on the surface of a stage
contrary to public comprehension
is known as dark without the truth
stabbed into a dream of glory
generously spilling from its jar

VI. Moods

Fatigue

And wham.
The whole of it whooshed.

Fatigue is a weasel
that softens the thoroughfare of energy
and marries the limbs;

limp, well-fixed, a spooky yielding.

A foible prelude to sleep,
an interlaced danger
to the so-called human with a well-groomed
weasel. The untamed couple battles

the immense face
to lay helpless on the pillow
and control all those little machines
in a whisper of closed eyelids;

their red, browns, and blue skies and the underside
of white dreams.

Full-bodied Laughter

I've got a lion-hearted laugh,
quite gigantic, celebrated even
more so than the spoil of you.
When you open your mouth
the way that you do,
I can shoot my full-bodied laughter
that will stick on your tongue like peanut butter.
I'm tempted to fool slowly around,
start with the laughter of a sweet rose, then I'll
build up to the mother-of-pearl, strung together until
my sides split wide
and a highly outlawed dinosaur lurches
jaws gaping, drool along the outer rim of its sharp, shrill cajole
torturing the plum from your veins
cuttingly crisscrossing
your embarrassed dapple skin
with its tic tac toe game
penetrating the last O,
round cherry moon faces in a row.
You'll be crucified with hardly an X;
you'll take up tap dancing,
ask your mother out for dinner
pay your alimony, send newsletters
of the success of your failure.
You'll snort and grunt
into your heart until the clam
opens and bleeds a river of fake smiles, until you
sew your lips and eyelids tight,
your ears plugged with anguish,
a stormy bellow and your body rests in
the pit of your soul;
a shallow and nervous pool.
I'm tempted to laugh you straight
into next spring, then fool slowly around
starting again with the laughter
of a sweet rose.

Her Hostile Oneness

the ship skipping kissed the ocean floor
a sand castle she became warm brown
and drifting off her nude lips
were the last remains of a voice

scattered helpless between her toes
crawling into the small spaces left
an unclean and dampened tongue with
fingertips that combed her matted mind

scorched her hostile oneness
a sea of potions flaming her thoughts
that swept the beast with a musing ebb
of a salty night upon her weary brow

Moment of Quietude

I thought I saw a gem
a highly prized moment
cut and polished
loved and specious
hanging loosely against my neck
light soaring from its center
time disappearing in its prism
so many transparent angles
so many worlds awaiting
slanting I'd been there before
decorative and gaudy in my sub-
conscious colors
distorted smiling refracting
good spirits from head to toe
beaming parallel
to myself roaming before
this place this space this
something fairly naive and uncommon
passionate gold chain
holding up such imminent passage
breaking in midstream
distorted smiling refracting
moment of quietude

Moods

It is wise to leave peaceful
the outstretched hands
of the woman's opening.

Like two feet; right and left
one in front of the other
treads
until one stride
is willfully trampled
in a wild marathon
with rubber souls to control the beast.

The road a light episode
after episode a brothel of actresses
in her hands
form a pool
a death throe he has
made an effort
to love and drink
the devil sir

part of her is gone

with one scene remaining
the ego from the forehead
the agony from the face
they both wait for the perverse beauty
and the fussing
to adjust

the tempo of the genius
coming not to rhyme
but to run home
after watching the petals fall
blown to the garden wall
will bloom another night.

Gently he'll smack his lips
every scented late hour
after work and a meal
in the unstill.

He'll dry the damp starlight
washed from the dark
of her crimson eye
shrinking
the wrinkled skin-crusted earth
beneath their dangling
tortured gaiety

entangled limbs crashing
through a planet of thoughts
distraught no more
off its course

hidden behind the shadows
of his heaving chest.

Tired with the tide
changed and thankful
waves in sets

smooths the surface
of their bodies

parting
her wet mouth
she hangs
on the neck of his spirit

and a vision spills
looking at the morning sun before it has risen

rightly
quieting temptations

covering them,
the hands of the woman's opening
and he is contentedly closed off now
always her whoring
to keep things
so she speaks no more of moods.

An Opaque Ritual

she can't take it so she blows
cigarette smoke into
wild animals, three rings and lions
three rings and camels, three
rings and ponies, she blows smoke-animals;
they twist and form the human rocket,
twist and form a human pretzel,
they fly on swings, on wires, on bits of
this and that, they blow away

jellylike white puffs, huge carnivorous beast-clouds
softening blows clown white blows
sarcastic greatest show cliché
daring her last breath, a coffee break feat
until nothing is left but circles of hooves
diminished in the clamor of an opaque ritual
melancholy smut shoveled by the stained wind

the crowd is in cunning dispersal
so she drags her last puff expanding her scorn
as if an anabolic steroid to the deflated muscle
and the depth of a slippery lung

she flexes her biceps while verbs
shatter the office walls when she enters
from her slow virus defeated
by the last clang of cymbals

Beyond Insanity

Embrace the transparent voices.
Believe what you hear
in the chaotic wind
curving inward

a deadly
swift crackling stream
stretches the vigor of your patience

until one last blossom
past the hoary posies
throngs past the powerlessness
of their powdery fuss.

Out pops the rosy cure
seemingly
venomous and unfaithful.
It smoothes the voices to capture
and toys with the daydreaming muse

tranquil and revolutionized
a capricious grace
a colorable red.

Of Vulgar Images

lollygagging Friday night kudos
and chili cheese curly fries
skies over Baghdad at Jimmy's
neck creaking to the reception
of vulgar images between bites
an antidote for chemicals
bodies strewn in blip
while inviolate cheerleader
eight year olds horselaugh
a sprouting yahoo cusses the corner
passing out over ice water
something in his red eyes
something primal and unloved
and soda and pastrami melts
down greasy chins before banana splits
slip into a coma puddle
screaming thoughts of marines
growing vines of Southern Iraq
heads down red light green light home
stomach aches sprout at midnight
veining subliminal reality
in a hothouse of sleep
and oil steeping the pores
inside I shoot the merging dark
thank you and amen good night

Wandering Furiously Inside

there's absolutely no scent
but the caress of mind
so hard is the night
wandering furiously inside
lonely takes his skin
rips it from the bone
and washes it in an ocean of appetite

that kisses the thought
slaps the torment from its want
melting any memories
beats it
holds it in its hole
smothering it in salty foam
eats away youth exhausted
in the midst of a surrealistic taking

coming into the light
on another day
it might have been *that* way
if it weren't *these* nights
with the mind
that isn't tormented by lust
and the malodorous animal that has growled past

becomes absolute and perfumed
without that thought
wandering in an inkling of circumspect
the thoughtless self
without the wet hard night

is a sweat soaked sheet
a tangible body of earth
covered in a watery dream
blowing coolly inland
premeditation

breezing into the hand of sky's future
the sun catches the surging
solitary eyes
and the lips from wave to wave
are a breath above

In The Length of a Moon-bathing Second

In the length of a moon-bathing second
madly following skeletonized footprints
I watched them fly
into a faraway jungle sky.

A straight line of insects stung by,
butterfly flutter, mysterious glowing
caught my mesmerized eye.

I dreamt I was delicate, a crawling thing
on the edge of a platonic friendship with tall plants
and grasses in vigorous flush
with an underweight flexible shape
planning to ignite, heavy lightning
fluorescence feverishly plucking it flown.

Trumpeting wishes for wings like complaint,
thin strips of leaves, a cocoon, a chrysalis,
sparkling silken strands, a web
in the length of a moon-bathing second,
stalking silhouettes emerge

disintegrate in a ripple of fog.
A line of traveling tracks monopolizing
the wet shore, straight dotted lines, four-footed
diagonal steps upward, a rare coincidence
toe drags and tail, an immobilized reptile.

Retreating, my bird-watching heart; streaks
of white spots gobbled by conspicuous blue.
Drawn to its watery realm, the refraction
of two eyes in a warping firmament.
A shore walker wading

from the firm-bottomed shallow mirror,
sand between toes, I dreamt
I was delicate, my body indent, my wing prints.

VII. Empowerment

Mirror Mirror Rebirth

She has been caressed
all her fair life, withdrawing into her chance
to reward the world
with a sacrifice, her limbs float
upstairs to the sun, her arms outstretched
she looses each moment before, ready to open

up from this underworld earth, kissing air
her mouth, the lips know without knowing
beforehand the song, her eyes accept
death, she has been stroked
for the light
her feet lightly on a new

tomorrow, to the gods she
rises upon each step undressing
as the priests take her hand
to take her heart, and on her last
step she trips without a voice
into a polished reflection

of sky twirling between her skin
and sacred mortal pain only the priests
that fall rapidly wild against the bloody night
can touch
as their hearts explode with fire
as the stairs crumble into a quiet exhale

and she reverses
before the disappearing mirror
a polished reflection arranged on an unfamiliar plane.

From a Slick Sexism

engaging clusters of contriving
men stand in a cool line
to watch the surrealistic
violently burning of a psychedelic poppy sun
the slack river of somnolent men
stream by comically
cold blue ice fizzing
their palms gently
swirling round and round
unburdening my breast?
dissolving tomorrow's hot-skin
to and fro gathered in steel gray
talking of yesterday
and blue skies
eyeing their tip of extreme coldness
hypnotizing the hysteria?
tornados of men touch
down crevices in the necks'
beaten dreams
scratching the navel
of future's natural scheme
breaking apart clumps of dirt
so erratically I climb
naked from the earth
tearing outdated roots attached to limbs
to become the centered velvet sun
psychedelic poppies burning
that violently scorched me
sleepily into one
hilarious triumph
"she is the one"
"she is the one" fantasy she is
again I am evolving
maybe only an inch taller
one step for women-kind-
flourishing-straightened
in a supernatural breath
and baby steps, baby steps
baby steps. I live for the greathearted affair

against a churlish dying repose
so yes I am, of course I am
the one hilarious triumph
I am me I am the one
and there are many like me

She Set Herself on Fire

She set herself on fire
to see her character flourish
dangerously happy
fulfilled completely flammable
mixing her ruddy complexion into a vivid hue.

A smoldering work of birth
the bashful pyromaniac admires the reflection
in everlasting smokey blue
satisfied with finicky life,
all mysterious tricks past.

She took noiseless match after noiseless match,
reached for invitations to rasp
to ignite, embracing optimistic kerosene
to press her lips to future's kiss
breathing in its tongue of flames.

Summons to Faith

I wish you self confidence
amidst the ignorant masses and chaotic winds of
society, there are
so few of your caliber, kindness
and reputable higher intellect

sent to this small town Earth in a galaxy
of supernatural change just to
make that subtle difference.
Only those with sight notice
the joy revealed the length
of your arm to student

which so many humans
aren't blessed
nor are they worthy of.

Please don't be done in
by sublimation for
world-weary is only a side affect
and retribution

is in the final document
how it is human nature to be flayed
by the very nature of our own human imperfections.
When so much rests

on the foundation
of theology
and your gentle lectures of experience,
knowledge and truth
riddle softly from your Christian spirit

while all the people gather round the spring
for the presence of
that humble virtue
we will sing let our people go!

Intensely Me

I crawled to my beginning out of liquid lungs
filled with high tide in an
unfathomable opening above, enfolding, churning
the hugeness of an undulating globe,

balanced my erect brothers and sisters
I am fair-minded surviving an enormity
above, enfolding, churning
the sheer size of a progressing orb.

My end together with this holy escape
from my ogling the high-ceilinged
beyond infinite universe to universe I voyage
the vastness of an ongoing bubble

my mind hurdled without emptiness
dreams spinning although I haven't found a purpose.
So I blemish the forces of perfection
like an imposing shadow in the excellence of light

sliding through what I was yesterday.
I won't be caught mortified in the face of death.
It only requests a starting point deep hole above I can
dive past; transforming, rising and falling intensely me.

Probably Mistaken For Feminism

She is swooningly animated;
a persuasive transport of syllables.
Slippery, glib verbs trickle.
Checkerboard nouns slide forward.
Blue adjectives linger
flirting
with a painful extraction

only now these phrases are self-satisfaction.
A syringe of morphine emotions
injected
poke at her primitive impulses.

Such overwhelming release
she molds *her stuff,*
channels
that belligerent tongue in her mind
that flippantly chatters.
Strings of suffering paragraphs

mingle at a party in her *new voice*
then dance the night away with a lack of control.
She leans to twirl freely
opinions and feelings on the page,
informs anyone of the candid facts

then sits merrily
until her endearing babbling
is suspended in a toothy smile;
probably mistaken for feminism
that is forgotten within the week.

Jesus Is a Woman

It's in their eyes.
I've seen it in a few
women in Algebra class
adding warmth and possibility.
Women in Literature class
stand tall sitting tired,
advantages in the sparkling
details in Botany, young middle-aged
older eyes describing
established criteria for working women
in the field of landscaping.

Jesus is a woman.
It's a second coming
dating back to Biblical times
beyond the essence of today's established methods,
beyond beaten down secretly, quietly
an old school under one law, free
beneficial progression.

Jesus is a woman.
In the eyes of women in my
short story class and my science lab,
none are exempt from responsibility,
some on Federal Student Aid,
state grants and loan programs.

It's in their eyes.
Jesus is a woman
of communication and achievement.
She's black and white but not yet read.
Her book is gray between the lines
that only she appreciates.
She's blue, red and white,
still misconstrued,
but the cross is in splinters
and the rock has been moved.

I Was My First Book

I was my first book.
I read many others but I was first.
Highly influenced by other books
mine was so typically me.
So I trashed it.
I scrapped it for a new one.
Of course, I kept pieces of the old one;
I know I kept some good pages.
What I didn't bargain for
were all those words written between
the lines, the ones I wasn't
aware of, sentences of steel,
smeared ink and resentment.
So, I went looking for the pages
I had torn into tiny fragments.
Piecing and sorting.
Sorting and piecing.
And over the flame
I heated the steel wool
and scrubbed any clandestine pessimism.
The steam rose fifty feet above my book.
Hiding from ones self,
although stealing isn't the thing
I stole myself back.
Like I said I was my first book.
Thank God I read some others.
As a fitful little drama
this book could sell.
I do feel sorry for this chimera
and the capricious characters I might reveal.

About The Author

Avoiding Confrontation By Writing Poetry is Victoria Hasenauer's first collection of poetry. Her poems illustrate a typical mother writing after the so-called "woman's work" is finished. At first, denial concerning confrontations in Victoria's life is repressed, and then expressed through inspired verse.

Victoria was born in Washington D.C. She lived most of her life in Los Angeles where she worked at her family's animal transportation business. She's the mother of three children, and she is now living in K.C. where she is working toward a Masters in Art Therapy.

inted in the United States
?LVS00006B/397-420